Jacquelin Ihuwan studied kinesiology at the University of Windsor, where she obtained a Bachelor of Human Kinetics in 2008. She then went on to obtain a Bachelor of Education from the University of Western Ontario in 2009 and is now a secondary school teacher. She currently lives in Windsor, Ontario, with her husband, and is the proud mother of two beautiful children. When she is not chasing her children around, you may find her out running, working on various art projects, or laughing with family and friends.

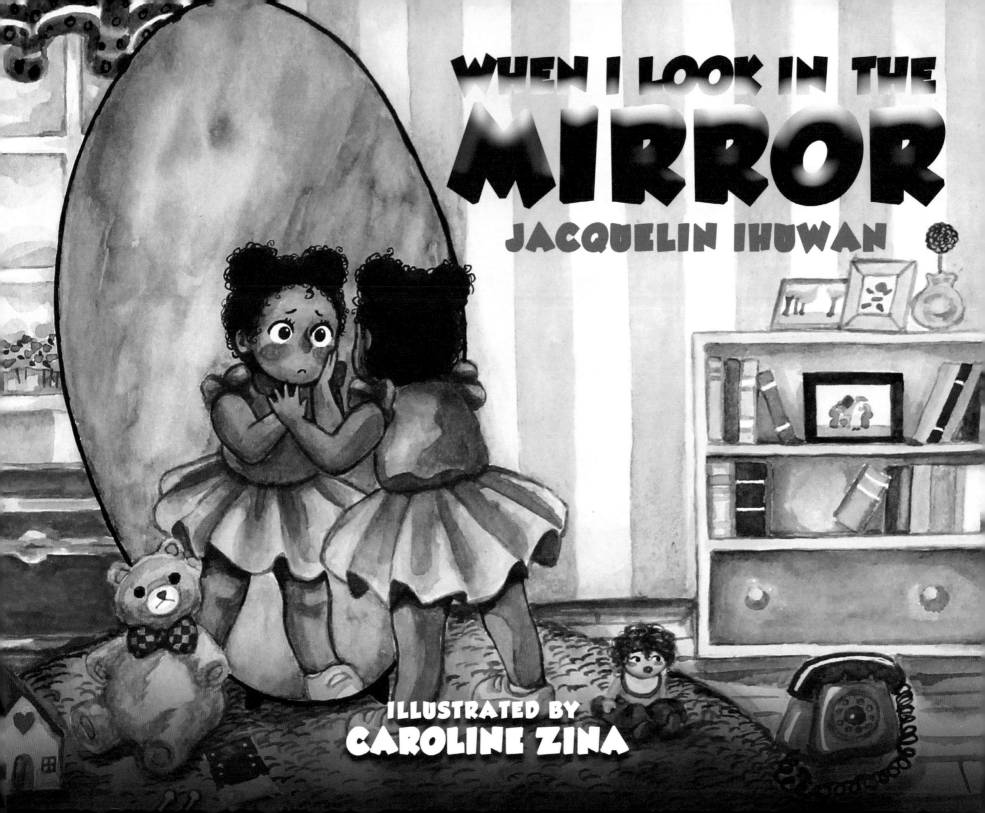

WHEN I LOOK IN THE MIRROR

JACQUELIN IHUWAN

ILLUSTRATED BY
CAROLINE ZINA

Copyright © Jacquelin Ihuwan (2020)

Illustrated by Caroline Zina

Ordering Information:
Quantity sales: special discounts are available on quantity purchases by corporations, associations, and others. For details, contact the publisher at the address below.

Publisher's Cataloging-in-Publication data
Ihuwan, Jacquelin
When I Look in the Mirror

ISBN 9781645750918 (Paperback)
ISBN 9781647505400 (ePub e-book)

Library of Congress Control Number: 2020912820

www.austinmacauley.com/us

First Published (2020)
Austin Macauley Publishers LLC
40 Wall Street, 28th Floor
New York, NY 10005
USA
mail-usa@austinmacauley.com
+1 (646) 5125767

To my children: May you feel nothing less than proud when you look in the mirror.

The completion of this story could not have happened without the constant love and encouragement from my husband, family, and one of my closest friends, Sarah. Thank you for your honesty, your patience, your feedback, and most importantly, for encouraging me to push myself beyond my comfort zone.

One summer day, while at the park, the other
kids that were there made a remark. They started
to question Talia about her mom and while it
truly upset her, she tried to remain calm.
"How is it possible that she's your mother? It is easy
to see that you aren't the same color."
"Of course, she is my Mommy," Talia began to yell.
"I don't understand why you can't tell!"

But when she got home and thought it through, her friends were right and she didn't know what to do.

There were plenty of things that no longer made sense. She needed some answers. She didn't like the suspense.

Later that night, while eating her food, Talia decided it was time; she was finally in the mood.

"Mommy, I have some questions that I need to ask, but answering these may not be an easy task."

"My eyes are brown, but yours are green. If they are not the same color, then what does that mean? When I look in the mirror, you're not who I see. Tell me Mommy, why don't you look like me?"

"My eyes are dark, just like Dad's. He and I look the same, does that make you sad? When I look in the mirror, Daddy is the only one I see. Please tell me Mommy, why don't you look like me?"

"My hair is
dark, but yours is
light. Your locks are straight,
and my curls are tight. When I look in
the mirror, you're not who I see. Tell me
Mommy, why don't you look like me?"

"My hair is coarse, and Dad's is the same. We both have hair that is impossible to tame. When I look in the mirror, Daddy is the only one I see. Please tell me Mommy, why don't you look like me?"

"When I look at my skin, it is nothing like yours. Your skin is light with freckles, and that's hard to ignore. When I look in the mirror, you're not who I see. Tell me Mommy, why don't you look like me?"

"Dad's skin is dark and though mine isn't the same, it is more like his, so how do you explain? When I look in the mirror, Daddy is the only one I see. Please tell me Mommy, why don't you look like me?"

Talia's mother was shocked and didn't know what to say. She wondered how long her daughter had felt this way.

She needed a moment to think it through, but after some time she knew what to do.

"Your physical looks do not make you my child. We are both high-energy; sometimes even wild. You're so full of life, with an infectious laugh. You are a social butterfly; you're my other half."

"Yes, Mommy and Daddy do look very different. You were made with love, and that's very apparent. You have traits from us both, like Daddy's eyes and my dimples, and when you start to laugh, like mine, your nose gets all crinkled."

"Ethnicity plays a role, and you have traits from the two. You're a perfect blend of us both, which makes you look like you. Being mixed is a blessing and although this is just the start, you cannot let other's comments tear you apart."

CPSIA information can be obtained at www.ICGtesting.com
Printed in the USA
LVIW010008100920
664724LV00002B/23